Evan lives with his family, Mama Dee and
Mama Gee and Anna Day, in apartment 2-D.

On Friday, Ileana comes for a sleepover.

She is Evan's best friend.

They have their favorite meal and watch
a dinosaur video.

The next day, Saturday, they have Oreos for a snack.

They taste better with a spoon.

Sunday morning is French toast time.

Evan helps his two mommies make the breakfast.

Anna Day has to go out for a walk. After the walk,
they will put up Evan's new tent.

One sock, two socks. Mama Gee watches.

Evan talks to Mama Dee while he puts on his shoes.

Evan plays with the tent's O-ring while Mama Dee
and Mama Gee put on their coats.

Out to the park...

...And back again, to put up his new birthday tent.

Tomorrow Evan will be four years old,

and the tent is his before-birthday present.

Mama Gee reads the directions. "I don't think we have the O-ring! The tent won't stay up without the O-ring."

Evan looks under the covers.

The O-ring is not there.

Anna Day watches Evan.

"Anna Day, do you have the O-ring?"

Evan looks under the table.

The O-ring is not there.

Anna Day rolls over.

Evan shouts, "Anna Day has the O-ring!"
Anna Day just looks.

The O-ring is found!

Now the tent can stay up!

Mama Gee slips the O-ring on the tent poles.

The tent is up!

Monday, Evan's birthday, is a school day.

Evan tells Jane and Patsy about the missing O-ring.

"Do you know where the O-ring was?

It was under Anna Day."

Evan tells Mark and Justin about Anna Day and
the O-ring. "Do you know where the O-ring was?
It was under..."

At his birthday party, Evan tells everyone about
Anna Day and the missing O-ring.

Every day for a long time, when Mama Dee and
Mama Gee and Anna Day and Evan go out for a walk,
they tell the story of Anna Day and the O-ring.